"Fawn," I begged, "please do something."

Fawn only shook her head. "If I let the wolf get away, my father will be angry with me. We trap animals because the white man gives us money for the skins. Our land has been taken away. The animals are all that are left to us."

Fawn's words made me angry. "I didn't take your land," I snapped. "My papa is helping to get it back."

The wolf lay very still, looking up at us with its green eyes. There was dried blood where the trap dug into its leg. I began to cry. Fawn picked up a dead branch. I covered my eyes so that I would not see her kill the wolf.

For Chris, Robin, Ron, Drew, Rex, and Sue,
and all my friends at the Petoskey library

Text copyright © 1997 by Gloria Whelan.
Illustrations copyright © 1997 by Tony Meers.

All rights reserved under International and Pan-American Copyright Conventions.
Published in the United States by Random House, Inc., New York, and
simultaneously in Canada by Random House of Canada Limited, Toronto.

http://www.randomhouse.com/

Library of Congress Cataloging-in-Publication Data
Whelan, Gloria. Shadow of the wolf / by Gloria Whelan ; illustrated by Tony Meers.
p.   cm.
"A Stepping Stone Book."
SUMMARY: In 1841 thirteen-year-old Libby and her family begin a new life on the
shores of Lake Michigan, where her father works as a surveyor for the Ottawa
Indians and Libby is reunited with her Indian friend Fawn.
ISBN 0-679-88108-5 (pbk.) — ISBN 0-679-98108-X (lib. bdg.)
[1. Ottawa Indians—Juvenile Fiction.   2. Ottawa Indians—Fiction.   3. Indians
of North America—Michigan—Fiction.   4. Frontier and pioneer life—Michigan—
Fiction.   5. Michigan—Fiction.]   I. Meers, Tony, ill.   II. Title.
PZ7.W5718Sh   1997   [Fic]—dc20   96-18652

Printed in the United States of America   10 9 8 7 6 5 4 3 2 1

Shadow
of the Wolf

by Gloria Whelan
illustrated by Tony Meers

A STEPPING STONE BOOK

Random House New York

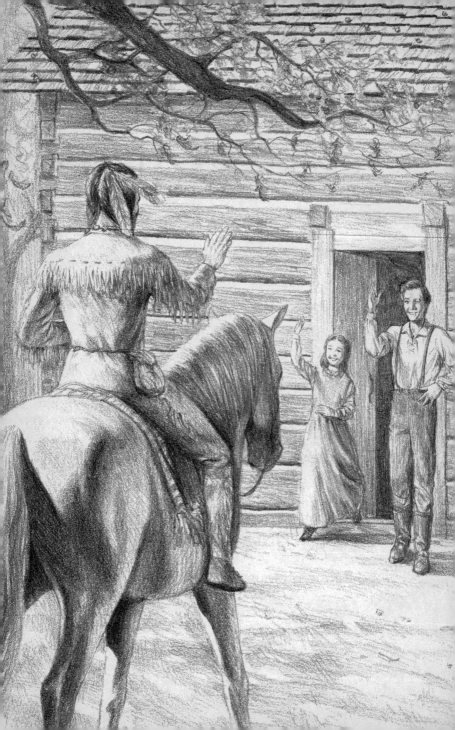

1

The September of 1841 arrived a red and gold leaf at a time. The ferns turned brown and shriveled. The falling acorns made little plopping sounds on the roof. One by one the singing birds left us until the woods were silent. Papa began to grow restless. That worried Mama.

With Papa there is no standing still. Even before our Potawatomi Indian friend, Sanatua, came, Papa was asking travelers about the northern woods. In our home of Saginaw, cabins had shot up everywhere. Papa is a surveyor who came to Michigan to measure out the miles of empty woods. Now there was little left to measure, and Papa was thinking about moving north.

A house had sprung up where I once picked blackberries. A family built on the opposite shore of the pond where I had spent many early mornings and evenings fishing. Their house stood where the blue heron used to nest.

I was excited when Sanatua came for Papa's help. "The Ottawa who have taken my family in have heavy troubles," he told us. "White men have come to buy up all the land around their village. One day the white men will cut down the trees. They say wood is needed to feed the bellies of the great steamships. They must have wood for building. In their villages, houses appear like mushrooms after an autumn rain."

"What will happen if the Ottawa lose that land?" Mama asked.

Sanatua frowned. "With no land on which to live, the Ottawa, like my own tribe, the

Potawatomi, will be sent far away."

"How can you stop these men?" Papa asked.

"Some years ago the Ottawa chiefs were deceived into selling much of their land to your government. In exchange, your government gives them money each year. The Ottawa can buy some of their land back, but it is not easy. The surveyors they hire cheat them. They take the best land for themselves. That is why I thought of you. You are a man the Ottawa could trust. But there is not much time. You once spoke of wanting to move north. Come and see our land. See if you would not be happy there."

Papa could hardly wait to saddle his horse and ride north with Sanatua. Mama and I stood by the window to watch them leave. I wanted to go along with them as far as the woods, for I can run as fast as Papa's horse can trot. But Mama would not let me. "You are thirteen now, Libby. Flying skirts don't become a young lady," she said.

It was hard for me to stand still when all my thoughts were traveling north with Papa. He would soon be seeing my dearest friend, Fawn. Fawn is Sanatua's daughter. In Indian her name is Taw cum e go qua.

In the distance Papa and Sanatua grew smaller and smaller. Soon they were gone altogether. Mama sighed and picked up William, who was beginning to cry. William is my year-old brother. I knew Mama held William not just because he was crying, but because he felt good. I used to hold my doll for the same reason when I was not so grown up as I am now.

I also knew that Mama did not want to leave Saginaw. Our small cabin was comfortable. We had cushions on the chairs and curtains on the windows. Mama had made a garden. The Maiden's Blush rosebush had been only a twig when we brought it from Virginia. This summer it had five blooms. Mama saved all the petals and put them in a bowl with spices.

I did not know how I felt about moving. Like Papa, I was sorry that the woods were disappearing from Saginaw. And if we went north, I would see Fawn. I had made friends in Saginaw, but none like Fawn. She was happy to watch a caterpillar on a leaf for five minutes at a time. Still, it was troublesome to think about going to unknown country.

While I waited for Papa to come back, I returned to my favorite places: the tall elm tree where the oriole had nested, the little stream where I had gathered tadpoles, and the stand of poplars where I used to hide in the early evenings to watch the beavers cut trees for their lodge.

When Papa returned three weeks later, he had a great surprise. He had bought a house in the northern woods! "We must hurry and pack our things," Papa said. "It will be a long trip on poor roads and the winter comes early there." We could see his heart had stayed in the north.

Mama bit her lip as she does when she is

unhappy. "Rob, we came all the way from Virginia to Michigan. Now, just as Saginaw is becoming settled, you want to take us away."

"Vinnie, I'm tired of living in a bundle, like squirrels packed into a hollow tree."

"But, Rob, our cabin is so comfortable."

"Wait until you hear about our new home. It was built for an American Fur Company trader. It has a kitchen and a parlor. Upstairs, there are two bedrooms." At that Mama looked happier. Our log cabin had only two small rooms.

"Papa," I asked, "would I have my own room?"

"Yes, Libby," said Papa, smiling, "but that is not the best of it. The house is on a bluff overlooking Lake Michigan. The lake is as big as a sea. And the lake is not like land that someone can buy and sell. It will always be there."

I was happy at the thought of a room of my own. I was even more excited to think that I would soon be seeing Fawn. When we parted, she had given me the silver eagle that she wore around her neck. "It will be as if you are one of our Eagle clan," she said. I had given her my bracelet with the tiny gold heart that had belonged to my grandmother.

Mama turned up her sleeves and I put on my oldest apron. Papa nailed together boxes to hold our possessions. We began to pack our things for the trip north.

Last to go in the wagon was William's cradle. It had been woven for him by Fawn's mother, Menisikwe. Around the top of the cradle was a border of sweet grass that made our whole wagon fragrant.

Eagerly, Papa coaxed our horses, Ned and Dan, onto the trail leading north. I could not help looking back. The sun was shining on our cabin. Geese and ducks were swimming on our pond. This year we would not watch them fly away as winter came. Instead, we were the ones to leave.

I began to understand how Fawn and the Potawatomi tribe had felt when they were forced to leave their village. I remembered how the women had cried out and the men had shouted angry words.

I had been there when it happened. I was visiting Fawn when the soldiers had come. Because I was wearing Fawn's clothes, the soldiers believed that I was an Indian, too. They meant to take all of the Potawatomi Indians to the empty country of the west. Sanatua and his family risked their lives to bring me back to Mama and Papa. Then they fled north to join the Ottawa. Now we were following in their footsteps.

2

There seemed to be no end to the trip. Each day, as dusk came, Papa would unhitch the wagon next to some small stream or lake. He would walk off into the woods with his musket in search of rabbits or squirrels for our dinner. I would gather firewood and Mama would put on a kettle of potatoes, carrots, and turnips.

At night Mama and I would make ourselves snug in the wagon. Papa would throw a quilt over a bed of pine branches and sleep under the sky. I tried it, but only for one night. The hooting of the owls and the cries of the wolves sounded much closer than they did in the wagon.

We spent hours in forests dark as the inside of a pocket. Then, suddenly, Ned and Dan would pull our wagon into a meadow that was filled with sun. We traveled through forests of pine trees so tall I could not see to the top of them. We came upon golden-leafed birch and sugar maples with leaves in every shade of red from scarlet to rust.

We forded streams and crossed rivers on log bridges. On wet days Ned and Dan struggled through mud. On dry days dust as fine as flour sifted onto everything. William fussed and cried because the wagon bumped so. Mama grew more and more silent. Papa tried to be cheerful for all of us. I could see, though, that he wished we would hurry and get there.

The closer we came to our new village of La Croix, the more Indians we saw. The men wore breechcloths and leggings that went from their ankles to their hips. Some had calico shirts embroidered with beads. They wore feathers in their hair or bright cloths wrapped around their heads. The women were in calico dresses or long tunics. Their leggings went only to the knee and were folded over at the top. Their hair was braided with ribbons or hung down with no ornament but a beaded band around their foreheads.

The Indians were curious about us. When we stopped in the evenings to camp, they peered into our wagon. Although Mama and Papa invited them to join us, they preferred to sit a little distance from our campfire, talking long into the night. What they liked best was William. The Indian women would pick him up from his cradle and pass him about, exclaiming at his bonnet and dress. When they first did this, Mama was frightened. But when she saw how carefully they held him and how they laughed at his gurgling, she forgot her worry.

We came to La Croix on a day so warm and sunny it was hard to believe it was the end of October. We saw a small mission church and next to it a great wooden cross, which gave the village its name. La Croix is French for "the cross." There was also a cooper's shop, where barrels were made for the fish the Indians caught and sold.

Scattered among the woods were two or three cabins. Through the trees we had our first glimpse of Lake Michigan. Along the shore of the lake were Indian wigwams with their coverings of birch bark or woven rush mats. Nearby were the fields where the Ottawa grew their corn. Beyond the fields were the Ottawa's burial grounds, with little birchbark houses to mark the graves. Two years before, Fawn's brother, along with hundreds of other Indians, had been carried off by the smallpox.

Sanatua greeted us. He told us that their chief was anxious to meet Papa. "Each day more land is eaten by these greedy men. But first you must take your family to your house. The tribe is thankful for your coming. They have brought wood so you will keep warm this winter. Here is maple syrup and a basket of fish for your dinner. Tomorrow I will come and take you to our chief."

"And Fawn?" I asked. "Will I see her?"

"Today Taw cum e go qua is gathering acorns with her mother. Tomorrow I will send her to you."

We left the village and once again entered the woods. After only a few miles we turned onto a road so narrow that the branches of the trees scraped against the sides of our wagon. I could see Mama was holding her breath. Suddenly, there in front of us was our house. Mama and I didn't wait for the wagon to stop. We jumped off. Mama ran toward the house. I ran toward the great Lake Michigan. Below me was a wide sand beach. Beyond the beach, as far as your eye could see, was the lake.

The ride that day had been hot and dusty. I took off my shoes and stockings. Then I gathered up my dress and ran down the bluff

and into the lake. I felt the wet sand between my toes. Gulls soared over my head. The cold waves slapped at my legs. As I looked over that endless water, the world seemed to grow.

Mama was calling to me. After I rubbed the sand from my feet, I hurried into the house. It looked enormous to me. Downstairs was a parlor with a large fireplace and a kitchen with another fireplace for cooking. There was one big bedroom for Mama, Papa, and William. I was to have the other bedroom. Because of the roof's pitch, you could only stand up in the middle of my room. But there was a window that looked out upon the lake and a door to close.

Mama was as pleased as I was. "Rob, I'm glad we came. The house needs a good cleaning, but when I hang our curtains and put down the rugs, we will have a fine home. And to have a lake right at our doorstep! Have you ever seen such a blue? Tomorrow I mean to get out my watercolors and paint the lake."

Papa laughed. "Why would you want to paint it, Vinnie, when you have it right here?"

I soon understood why Mama wanted to paint the lake, for it was forever changing. If you did not catch the lake's color or the way the sun shone on it, the color and the dazzle would be lost forever.

That evening a rain began to fall, and we quickly got to know the house better. The roof leaked, so we had to put pails in the bedrooms to catch the water. Every cupboard we opened showed that mice lived in the house. When we lit a fire, the chimney smoked so badly we had to open all the windows and doors, inviting the storm inside.

Papa promised to clean the chimneys and patch the roof first thing in the morning. Mama scrubbed the cupboards and scolded the mice out of the house. We made a fine dinner of the fish Sanatua had given us. Mama cooked up some apples we had brought from Saginaw, and we each had a bit of the maple syrup on them. We had just finished our dinner when we heard a knock at our door.

3

The man at the door had no more shape than a dumpling. You had to search for his eyes and nose and mouth in all the folds of his skin. He was gasping for breath from the effort of riding his horse to our house. When Mama offered him a chair, he sank down upon it.

Finally he was able to speak. His name was George Blanker, he said. He was dressed in a fine suit and tall hat. In his hands he held a box, which he now handed to me. "Here you are, little girl, a small present."

I carefully lifted the lid of the box. Inside

was a doll more beautiful than I could ever have imagined. She had a china head with pink cheeks, real hair, and blue eyes that seemed to look right at me. She was dressed in silk and even wore tiny leather shoes. I exclaimed with pleasure.

Papa looked less pleased. "That's very kind of you, sir, but it is a more generous gift than we would expect from a stranger."

I gave Papa a questioning look. Mr.

Blanker cleared his throat. "Mr. Mitchell, sir, I hope we will soon be friends rather than strangers. I understand you are a surveyor. Our company is in need of one. I can promise we will pay you well."

"What is your company, sir?" Papa asked.

"Why, I represent one of the largest timber companies in the state of Michigan. We own thousands of acres. We are logging downstate now. But we want to have a new supply of forest ready and waiting. If you don't buy ahead, the price becomes too dear. There is a fine harbor just south of here where steamers can load the logs and take them down to Chicago. They say houses are rising there at the rate of one a day."

Papa's lips tightened. "Where will this land come from?"

"Why, from the Indians!" Mr. Blanker looked pleased with himself. "According to the Treaty of 1836, the government has the right to take back the land around here that the Ottawa Indians have been living on. We mean to buy up that land. And I will tell you a secret." He lowered his voice and looked about as though there might be spies in the room. "I have heard that there is a grove of bird's-eye maple around here. I mean to have it. Bird's-eye is all the thing for furniture."

Mama has often enough told me that children should be seen and not heard. Still, I could not help asking, "What if the *Indians* want to buy back their land?"

Mr. Blanker gave me a surprised look, as if a dog had suddenly started talking. Then he appeared cross. Finally he laughed.

"Well, miss, we are going to get there first. We're a lot shrewder at buying land than the Indians. Let them go up to Canada or out west. Why, I heard only the other day that those Indians want the government to give them citizenship status. They want to be able to vote. What do you say to that?"

Mama sat up very straight in her chair. She reached over and took the doll from me. Carefully she wrapped the doll up and placed her back in her box. Then she handed the box to Mr. Blanker.

"What's this?" he said.

Papa stood up. "I'm afraid I have already pledged to work for someone else."

"Someone else? Tell me what that company has agreed to pay you and I will double it."

"There is no company," Papa said. "I have come north to survey land for the Ottawa and to help them buy back as much land as they need."

All the folds on Mr. Blanker's face puffed out like the cheeks of a frog. "You will never get rich working for Indians."

"It was never my plan to get rich, Mr. Blanker. I only wanted to help the Indians, who are my friends. Now I have another purpose. It is to see that you do not get the land. Good day, sir."

The door slammed as Mr. Blanker stamped out of the house.

"Who was that man?" I asked.

"He is what is called a timber cruiser," Papa said. "Such men go about scouting large sections of land for logging companies."

Mama sighed. "We have been here less than a day and already we have an enemy."

"We have right on our side, Vinnie. That is all the protection we need."

I told myself Mama had been right to give back the doll. Still, my arms felt empty. I knew I would never see such a doll again. It was wrong, but I would have given up many trees to keep her. The loneliness of this strange, new place made me long for something of my own to hold on to.

We were all too tired from our travels to let Mr. Blanker's rudeness keep us awake. For the first time in his life William slept through the night. Papa said the sound of the waves soothed him. Indeed, the washing of the waves against the shore is the most restful sound you can imagine. Somewhere between one wave and another I fell asleep.

4

Papa worked on the roof all the next day. When he finally came in to supper, he had a present for me. "It's not a fancy doll, Libby, but it will be company for you." He handed me his handkerchief, which he had knotted into a kind of little bag. I nearly dropped the handkerchief—it was moving! Papa told me to untie the knots.

As soon as the first knot was undone, I saw big brown eyes staring out at me. Hastily, I untied the other knots.

"It's a flying squirrel, Libby. There was a nest of them in the chimney. The other squirrels got away, but this one seemed tame."

The squirrel was so tiny he fit into the palm of my hand. His fur was brown on top and white underneath. On either side was a fold of skin reaching from his front to his back leg. Papa said the folds stretched out like wings so the squirrel could glide from tree to tree. His feathery tail curved over his body like a plume. He had enormous brown eyes, shiny as acorns. "That's so the squirrel can see at night," Papa said.

"Can I keep it?" I asked. I was afraid that, like the doll, he might be snatched from me.

"Yes, Libby," Papa said, "as long as you take good care of the creature."

"Can he stay in my room at night?"

"He can," Papa laughed, "but you may be sorry." He wouldn't tell me why.

When it was time for bed, I closed the door so the squirrel couldn't get away. I placed him carefully on my dresser in a little nest made from my hankies. In the blink of an eye, he glided from the dresser to the

rafter. From the rafter he dropped down to the bedstead. From the bedstead he swooped to the chair. He wouldn't stay still. All night long I heard him gliding about the room, so that I hardly slept. In the morning I found him curled up asleep in my shoe.

Papa explained that flying squirrels only go about at night. "They rest during the day. I think if you want any sleep at night, I had better build a cage for the squirrel. What will you call him?"

"Icarus," I said. Mama had taught me the story of the boy who tried to escape from the Greek island of Crete by fashioning wings of feathers and wax. He could fly at night, but when daylight came, he flew too close to the sun. His wings melted and he fell into the sea.

Early the next morning Fawn walked through the front door without a sound. Papa says if she had a mind to, Fawn could walk up to a deer without scaring it away. Over a year had passed since Fawn and I had seen each other. Her hair was braided now, like a young woman's. She was no taller than I, but somehow she seemed older.

We were quiet at first, but then words came tumbling out. We both talked at once, hurrying to tell one another all that had happened in the last year. Soon it felt as if no time had passed at all.

"I must return to the village now," said Fawn at last. "This morning we take up our fish nets. Would you like to come and help us? It is women's work and you would be welcome."

Papa said, "I'm going to the Indian village this morning to meet the chief. I can take the two of you with me in the wagon."

At the Indian village Fawn's mother, Menisikwe, welcomed me. Fawn's little brother, Megisi, who is just William's age, was strapped to Menisikwe's back in a cradleboard. Megisi wore no clothes. Instead, he was surrounded with lichen, which the Indians first softened and then used like a diaper. When it was soiled, you had only to throw it away. When she was washing William's diapers, Mama often said that the Indians had a better idea.

The women tucked up their skirts and waded into the lake. Nets fashioned of basswood twine had been put out the night before and fastened to poles stuck in the lake bottom. As the nets were pulled up, I could see hundreds of wriggling fish caught in the mesh. The women dragged the nets onto the

shore with much laughing and shouting. They freed the fish and placed them in large birch-bark baskets. Most of the fish were what our French Canadian neighbors in Saginaw had called *poisson blanc*, or whitefish.

I tried to help, although Fawn freed five fish to my one. Sometimes one of the women who had pulled loose a large fish would throw it at a friend, giggling as the woman

tried to catch the slippery fish. The fish, laid out across racks to dry in the sun, would be food for the winter.

At noon I shared a bowl of corn soup with Fawn. In the afternoon we dug up potatoes and beets. At last Menisikwe said that Fawn might leave her work for a little, and the two of us walked along the shore of the lake.

The shore was covered with gifts. There were stiff white gull feathers, clamshells whose insides were like pearl, and stones in every shade of pink and green. What we liked best of all were the pieces of driftwood worn by water and wind into strange shapes. We took turns guessing what each piece of driftwood looked like—a bear, a turtle, a boat?

By the time we returned to the village, Papa was ready to leave. There was a serious look on his face. We heard him talking in a low voice to Sanatua. "Those men will stop at nothing to get the land the Ottawa wish to buy. But I do not mean to let them have it."

I was glad Papa was standing up for the Indians, but I could not help feeling worried, for I remembered how angry Mr. Blanker had been with Papa. As I said good-bye to Fawn, I could see that Papa's words had troubled her as well. "You won't have to go away again, will you?" I whispered. She only shook her head.

5

Each morning Mama would set lessons for me. As soon as my work was finished, I would climb into the wagon and drive with Papa to the Indian village. There I would help Fawn with her tasks. We would go into the woods to find firewood. We sat cross-legged for long hours while Menisikwe showed us how to weave mats to cover the wigwams. We hunched over buckskin shirts, embroidering them with beads. We wove rawhide into a frame of ash to make snowshoes.

The snowshoes were shaped like a bear's paw. They were painted in bright colors and decorated with tassels.

Menisikwe made Fawn do over anything that was not perfectly done the first time. When I made a mistake, Menisikwe was more patient. I think she expected less of me because I was not an Indian.

Sometimes Fawn's face clouded over when her mother scolded. She looked as if she would like to answer back. Yet she never did. Once when we were alone, I asked, "Why is your mother so strict?"

Fawn sighed. "If a snowshoe breaks miles from our village, someone may freeze to death. If a heavy snow comes and we have not gathered enough wood, the tribe may die of the cold. We cannot be careless in anything we do."

Papa spent many days meeting with Chief Ke che oh caw. They were making plans to buy a piece of woodland near the Indians' village. The land had the maple trees needed to make syrup. It was also good hunting land for grouse and pigeon. There was a small lake that would provide fish and ducks and a meadow where corn could be grown. It was the same land that Mr. Blanker wanted to buy.

Papa said Fawn and I might go with him on the day he was to begin surveying the woodland. He left us at the small lake and went off to mark the boundaries of the property. "I'll be back in an hour or two," he told us. "Stay by the lake and don't go wandering off."

Mama had given us bread and smoked ham, and Menisikwe had sent along a basket of dried blueberries. That morning there had been a frost. The grass had stood stiff and white. Now a warm sun was making the frost disappear. We settled under a maple tree. Its leaves were so red that in the sun it looked as if it was on fire. One by one the leaves fell slowly into our laps. We were choosing the showiest ones when we heard a strange noise overhead. It was a high-pitched *whooo, whooo.* The next minute there was a noisy flutter, and a dozen great white birds alighted on the lake. They were swans.

Fawn and I held our breath as the swans moved over the water, making soft whistling sounds. All at once they took off in a great commotion. Something had startled them. A minute later we heard voices. At first I thought it might be Papa coming back sooner than he had planned. Fawn shook her head. In a moment she was scrambling up into the branches of the maple tree. She motioned me to follow. The branches were low and close to one another, like steps. In no time we were high up off the ground.

A wagon made its way around the shore of the lake. Two men climbed down from the wagon. One of the men was Mr. Blanker. His companion was a big man with broad shoulders and arms like tree trunks. "You can be sure this is a grove of bird's-eye maple," Mr. Blanker said. "I cut down just such a tree here last summer. That man, Mitchell, will be surveying here for the Indians any day now. If we want these trees, we'll have to hurry."

The other man shook his head. "There's a risk. This land don't belong to you. I'll be needing a little extra money to calm my nerves."

"You do your job and you'll get your money."

The two men dragged a great crosscut saw from their wagon. They walked toward our tree. We heard the rasp of the saw as it was drawn across the tree. Fawn grabbed my arm. "Do what I do," she whispered. She let out a bloodcurdling howl. I did the same.

"Indians!" the men shouted. "The trees are full of them!" They dropped their saw and ran toward their wagon. In seconds they were gone.

We had to wait up in the tree for nearly an hour before Papa came back. All the while we were afraid that the men would return for their saw. When we told him what had happened, Papa looked worried. "I should never have left you girls here alone."

The worry changed to a smile as we described how our howls had frightened the two men into running off and leaving their saw behind. "Well, Libby," he said. "You and Fawn were very brave. And Sanatua was saying only yesterday it would be a great help to the Indians if they had a crosscut saw! It would make it easier to get firewood. We can tell him that you and Fawn arranged for Mr. Blanker to lend him one."

I would have sat up in the tree for another hour to hear such praise from Papa.

6

That same week Fawn and I had our first argument. We were in the woods gathering acorns. I wanted them for Icarus. Fawn was gathering them for her mother, who would pound them into flour. Fawn and I tried to catch tumbling oak leaves. They were the very last leaves to fall from the trees. We would reach for a leaf, sure that this time we would catch it. We never did. Moving a hand through the air made the light leaf change direction. The leaf floated out of reach. We might as well have tried to catch a falling star.

We were laughing at how foolish we

looked when we heard a strange sound, like a child whining. We stood perfectly still. The cry came again, this time like a howl. It sounded close by. We looked all around us. Then we saw, almost hidden by leaves, a struggling animal. Its leg was caught in the steel jaws of a trap.

"It's a dog!" I said.

"No," Fawn said. "It is a wolf. And the trap has my father's trap mark on it. We must find a log and kill the wolf."

I was horrified. "You can't do that! We have to let it go."

Fawn looked at me as though I had lost my mind. "Why should I let it go? There will be money from the wolf's fur and a bounty as well. We need the money to buy seeds for next spring's planting."

I paid no attention to Fawn. I was on my knees trying to figure out how I could release the wolf. At first I had been afraid that the wolf would bite me with its sharp white teeth, but it seemed to know I wanted to help it. "Fawn," I begged, "please do something. You know how this trap works."

Fawn only shook her head. "If I let the wolf get away, my father will be angry with me. We trap animals because the white man gives us money for the skins. Our land has been taken away. The animals are all that are left to us."

Fawn's words made me angry. "I didn't take your land," I snapped. "My papa is helping to get it back."

The wolf lay very still, looking up at us with its green eyes. There was dried blood where the trap dug into its leg. I began to cry. Fawn picked up a dead branch. I covered my eyes so that I would not see her kill the wolf. When I opened them, I saw that she was using the branch to pry apart the trap. Gently, she released the wolf's leg. "You must tell no one what I have done," she said to me.

Eagerly I promised. Together we watched the wolf. At first it just lay there licking its foot. I had never seen a wolf that close before. Warily, I reached my hand out and ran it over the wolf's soft coat. The wolf licked my hand. I was not sure I liked my hand being that close to the wolf's sharp teeth, but nothing happened. Still, there was something frightening and mysterious in being so close to a wild animal.

We watched as the wolf gathered its strength and struggled to its feet. It stood for several minutes, holding up its injured foot. Slowly, the wolf hobbled away into the woods. Twice it stopped and looked back at us. Soon it was lost among the trees and tall grasses.

I was careful not to give away our secret. But that night I had a question for Papa. "How can the Indians use cruel traps with steel teeth?"

"Once the Indians used a different kind of trap," Papa said. "Poles were pounded into the ground to make a circle. In the middle was an opening. When the animal walked into the opening and began to eat the bait, a board was released that closed off the entrance. But now the traders sell traps with steel teeth to the Indians."

That night I dreamed of the wolf. In my dream the wolf had no injured foot. It bounded through the woods, nimble and happy and free.

7

Winter rushed in across Lake Michigan. An angry wind blew off the lake day and night. It shook the house and rattled the windows. When I went down to the lake for a pail of water, I had to hang on to the trees to keep from being blown away. Snow hid everything. The trail to our house had disappeared.

Papa had to put runners on our wagon so that we could go to La Croix for supplies. At the cooper's shop you could buy not only barrels but flour and salt and potatoes. The cooper, Mr. Rouge, even had a few lengths of cloth. Papa placed me in the sleigh between him and Mama. William was wrapped so tightly in a blanket that all you could see of him was his nose.

Our horses, Ned and Dan, stepped through the snow. Their breath came out in clouds of steam. The trees wore armfuls of snow on their branches. As we brushed against the branches, the snow tumbled down on us. Snow birds fluttered up, white and quick, like the flakes that flew around us.

As we passed the Indian village, I thought of Fawn. I had not seen her since we had let the wolf go. If it weren't for the smoke escaping through the holes in the wigwams, you would think the Indian village deserted. The men were out hunting and minding their trap lines. Fishing had all but stopped. When the nets were pulled up, the fish froze right in the mesh. The women were in their wigwams, preparing the few animal skins that the men had been able to bring home. Game was becoming scarce. I thought of how welcome the wolfskin would have been. Sanatua had told Papa that soon the Indians would have to make their living as farmers. It was more important than ever that Papa help them to buy back their land.

At last we reached Mr. Rouge's cooper's shop, a small log cabin near La Croix's great cross and church. *Rouge* means "red" in French, and the name fit the cooper very well. He was a great hunk of a man with a ruddy complexion and a red nose shaped like the beak of a hawk. He made us very welcome, urging us to take the seats next to the stove. He bustled about, taking our wraps and handing out mugs of hot cider.

Mr. Rouge's two boys helped in the shop. They were twins, two years older than I. Their names were André and François. They were tall and slim, with faces still brown from the summer. Their black hair was slicked back with some sort of grease. They wore identical shirts and trousers. "Bet you can't tell which of us is which," André said to me. I looked very hard at them and could not.

The twins opened their mouths and gave me wide smiles. I thought that was odd, but I smiled back anyway.

"No," François said. "That's how you tell us apart."

When I looked again, I saw that François had a gap between his front teeth. André did not. "What if you aren't smiling?" I asked.

Mr. Rouge laughed. "Ah, but my boys are

happy creatures. They smile all the time."

The twins appeared good-natured. Still, there was a great deal of snickering and poking between them. "You must excuse my boys' manners," Mr. Rouge said. "They don't know how to behave in front of a young lady. You have the lads all aflutter."

At this there was even more snickering and poking. I blushed. I had no wish to agitate the twins. In fact, I heartily wished that they would just disappear.

While we were talking, a hen ran into the room. Mrs. Rouge hurried after it. She was a small neat woman, as plump as her chicken. She apologized. "I keep the chickens in our storeroom in the winter." After a chase, the hen was rounded up and closed in with the other chickens.

Before we left, Mama and Papa invited the Rouges to come and spend Christmas Day with us. A whole day with the twins! I did not see how I could stand it.

8

Because we were so busy preparing for winter, there had been no time to see Fawn. I begged Papa to take me along with him on his next trip to the Indian village. Papa was helping the Indians petition the United States Government to allow them to become citizens of America. They wished to vote and to have the protection of the law. Papa and Chief Ke che oh caw were going to ask other chiefs to join the La Croix tribe in their petition.

"Do you think our government will listen to you and let the Indians vote, Papa?" I asked.

"Not this year, Libby, but surely one day it must come about."

Mama had a sly smile on her face. "When it does, Rob, you must also ask them to let women vote."

Papa shook his head. "You can't be serious, Vinnie. That day will never come."

When we arrived at the Indian village, I ran to find Fawn. She was standing at the entrance of her wigwam wearing the snowshoes we had made. "I am going to find some wood for the fire," Fawn said. "Winter has come so early this year. Our wood may not last."

"I'll come with you," I said.

Fawn went to borrow snowshoes for me. When she returned, she helped me strap them onto my boots. At first I stumbled with every step. But Fawn showed me how to lift one snowshoe over the other, and soon I was stepping lightly over the snowdrifts. It was a strange feeling, for I was walking over the tops of grasses and shrubs buried under the snow. We each carried a basket on our backs to hold the wood.

There was so much snow on the ground that the only wood we could find was dead branches in the trees. Looking for branches we could reach, we kept walking farther into the woods. At last our baskets were full and we turned back toward the village.

We had been so busy that we had not noticed the sun disappearing and the snow starting up. Now the sky was a whirlwind of white. The snow got in my mouth and nose and eyes. My eyelashes were so fringed with flakes I could hardly see. Because the snow was wet, it formed clods and crusts on our snowshoes, making them heavy to lift. The snow covered our tracks as soon as we made them. We thought we were going in the direction of the village, but nothing looked as we remembered.

I turned to Fawn. She was so much at home in the woods, I was sure she would know the direction to the Indian village. But

Fawn only looked puzzled. "The snow has changed everything," she said. In the few minutes we had been standing still, the snow had nearly covered us. I was warmly dressed, but Fawn had only a blanket wrapped over her thin calico shift to keep her warm. Her thick black hair was coated with snow. It looked as if she was wearing a white cap. Her hands were thrust inside the blanket to keep them warm. I wanted to give her my scarf and one of my mittens, but she would not take them.

We thought someone might be within calling distance. Together we shouted into the storm. Only the wind answered. "If I could see the sun, I could find my way," said Fawn. But the sky was tumbled with dark clouds. And the farther we went, the more uncertain we became.

Just ahead, a gray shadow moved across the snow. It looked like the figure of a wolf! Papa said wolves did not attack human beings. Still, Papa might be wrong. I was relieved to see the shadow turn and lope away in the opposite direction. But when we hurried away, the wolf ran back toward us. It had a limp.

"Fawn!" I exclaimed. "It's *our* wolf! Why is it running back and forth?"

"I think it wants us to follow," Fawn said. And indeed the wolf kept running toward us and turning back in the other direction. It seemed to be telling us to come with it. "I think we should do as the wolf wishes," Fawn said.

"What if it is the wrong way?" I asked. "We will go deeper and deeper into the woods and no one will ever find us."

"We must trust the wolf," Fawn said.

"You wanted to kill it," I could not help reminding her, "and now you want to risk our lives by following it."

"The wolf is grateful," Fawn said. "We must go where it wants to take us."

Reluctantly, I turned around and we began to follow the wolf. It now limped

ahead, no longer looking back at us.

"What if it's just leading us to its pack and they eat us up?" I asked. Yet as we hurried after the wolf, the woods began to look more familiar. At last we saw smoke rising from the village campfires in the distance. We could hear Papa calling to us. He and Sanatua had come to look for us. The wolf turned and disappeared, its gray shadow vanishing into the white of the storm.

Papa hugged me. Sanatua took Fawn's

hand and led us toward his wigwam and the warm fire inside. Fawn had warned me to say nothing of how we had rescued the wolf from her father's trap. Now it was she who told the story. Sanatua listened carefully. When Fawn had finished, he spoke. "It was the body of the wolf I caught in my trap, but it was the spirit of the wolf you released. Perhaps it was its spirit who guided you home."

I was sure it was just a wolf we had seen, but I could not forget Sanatua's words.

9

Two days before Christmas it started snowing again. At first it was only glitter in the sun. But soon the flakes were as large as silver dollars. On Christmas Eve a wind started up. When you looked out the window, all you could see was a white blur. The Rouges would never be able to get to our house for Christmas. The blizzard would keep them away.

Earlier in the week I had gone with Papa to choose a Christmas tree. Now Papa brought it in. Our whole house was filled with the scent of pine. Mama had made paper angels to hang on the tree. I colored the angels and strung ropes of dried berries. We sat up late on Christmas Eve, admiring the tree in the firelight and listening to the wind trying to get inside. Icarus was just as pleased with the tree as we were. He glided to the top of the tree and down again. He thought a tree in the house was the most natural thing in the world.

When I awakened Christmas morning, the snow hung down from the roof so far that I could not see out my window. There was no heat in my room so I had to bring my clothes under the bed quilts to put them on. Mama was already in the kitchen fixing breakfast. William was chewing on the dried blueberries Mama meant to put in the pancakes. Papa had set a crackling fire. On the table were six presents. I added two more.

"The storm will surely keep the Rouges from joining us," Mama said. I could tell that she was disappointed. "I've been cooking all week to give them a good dinner."

After breakfast Papa read the Christmas story from the big family Bible. Finally it was time for the presents. I went first. Papa had carved a doll for me! Mama had sewn a dress and bonnet for the doll. There was a pretty dress for me as well. Mama had made it from a pale blue calico with dark blue flowers.

William's present was a set of wooden blocks that Papa had made. Mama had carefully painted the letters of the alphabet on the blocks. Papa's gift to Mama was a shelf for her spices. He had put fancy carving all around it. Mama had knitted Papa a sweater from wool she had unraveled from an old blanket. I gave Mama a needle case I had patched together. For Papa I had baked his favorite molasses cookies.

We were admiring the presents when we heard a stirring outside. The next moment the door was flung open. It was the Rouges! They hurried through the door, scattering snow everywhere. Mama was so happy that she threw her arms around Mrs. Rouge.

"Merry Christmas!" Mr. Rouge called out. "Our wagon was stuck in your trail so we just unhitched the horses and left it there. May we stable the horses in your barn?"

As soon as the horses were taken care of, we listened to Mr. Rouge's story of their travels through the storm. "There was nothing but white out there. But once I say I will be there, you can count on me."

Mrs. Rouge was a woman who would not sit still. In no time she was in the kitchen with Mama, a towel knotted about her waist. Mr. Rouge and Papa were jumping up and down on the parlor floor, judging whether it needed new supports to strengthen it. I showed Icarus to the twins. He was sound asleep. François poked him to wake him up, but he only went right back to sleep. "When evening comes," I promised, "we'll let him out of his cage and he'll glide up and down the Christmas tree."

I soon found that François and André could not bear to be in the house for two minutes together. They looked out of the window. They stuck their heads out of the door, letting in a whirlwind of snow. At last they could stand it no longer, and they wound their scarfs around their heads and plunged outside. Mama did not want me to go out into the storm. I was allowed to follow the boys only after promising many times that I would stay within sight of the house.

André and François found a barrel and took turns pushing one another over the bank that led down to the lake. Their bloodcurdling screams echoed all the way down. They invited me to fold myself into the barrel and take a turn. At first I was afraid. But when they promised to push me down an easy slope, I agreed. I was happy to find that, although they were rough with each other, they were gentle with me.

We were snapping off the icicles from the house and licking them when Mama called us in for dinner. We had wild turkey and sweet potatoes cooked with maple syrup, carrots, parsnips, thick slabs of cornbread, and, for dessert, a Christmas cake with raisins and walnuts. It was the only time I did not see François and André smiling—their mouths were too full!

After supper I let Icarus out of his cage. André and François thought the flying squirrel the best thing they had ever seen. They were eager to imitate Icarus's flights. It was only their mother's scolding that kept them from climbing up onto the furniture and plunging to the floor.

Because of the storm the Rouges were with us for two days. All the while the house was full of excitement and laughter. At first I thought the twins created only noise and confusion. But then I began to notice other things. They were tender with Icarus. And while they did not always listen to their papa, they did as their mama told them. I was truly sorry to see the Rouge family leave.

10

By the end of winter the Indians had saved
enough money to buy the piece of land that
Papa had surveyed. The head of each family
would contribute part of the money they had
received from the government. The money
was a payment for lands that had been taken
from the Indians. Now they could buy back
some of that land. Two days before the
papers were to be signed, everything
changed. Five Ottawa families announced
that they were leaving. Without their share of
money there would not be enough to purchase the land.

The spokesman for the five was a young man named Ke che gaw baw, the eldest son of one of the families. "The white man will take more and more of the land around us," he said. "Soon there will be no animals left to hunt. We do not wish to be farmers and do women's work. We wish to stay hunters. After the boiling of the maple sap is over, we will travel north to the greatest of all the lakes, Kitchi-Gami. That is where we will make our new home."

Papa and I were in the Indian village at the end of March when the five Ottawa families walked away from the camp. They took all they owned with them. Even the children carried small bundles on their backs. I had heard angry words said against them. Still, when they left, all the members of the tribe came to see them off.

"What will happen now?" I asked Papa.

"Mr. Blanker will try to get the land."

Sanatua sighed. "If that man would take a part of the land," he said, "we would have enough to pay for what is left."

Papa shook his head. "I'm afraid he would never be satisfied with only part."

Suddenly I remembered something. I told Papa and Sanatua how Fawn and I had overheard Mr. Blanker. He had said that he wanted the grove of maples because he believed they were bird's-eye maples. "What does bird's-eye maple look like?" I asked.

Papa said, "The grain of the wood looks as if it has a thousand little eyes. Almost all the bird's-eye maple trees are here in northern Michigan. The wood from them is rare and sells at a high price."

"The man is very foolish," Sanatua said. "There is no knowing whether you have such a tree until it is cut down."

"But he doesn't know that," I said. "So he might be happy with the land around that grove."

A smile began to grow on Papa's face. "Well, Libby," he said. "Your idea might just work."

The tribe called a council, and agreed that Mr. Blanker should be allowed to buy the grove. The sale would give the tribe enough money to buy the rest of the land!

Mr. Blanker jumped at the offer. He acted as if he had made a fine bargain. With great ceremony Papa and Sanatua and the chief of the tribe traveled to La Croix. They proudly registered their purchase of the rest of the land.

The trouble was that no one trusted Mr. Blanker to keep to his agreement. If he found that there were no bird's-eye maples on his land, he might become angry and cut down trees on the Indians' property.

Papa had an idea. "I know how we can protect the trees," he said.

When the day came, all of the members of the tribe filed into the woods that now belonged to the Indians. Every man, woman, and child stood next to a tree. The Indians let Papa stand next to a large oak tree. Fawn and I stood beside two small beech saplings. Only the maples in Mr. Blanker's grove were unattended. We all stood silently, waiting.

At last Mr. Blanker and several other men pulled up in a wagon. We were so quiet that at first they did not see us. When they did, they jumped right up into the air. But Mr. Blanker had paid for his land and he meant to have his trees. One by one the great maples fell. The limbs were sawed off and the logs hoisted onto the wagon.

When the grove was cleared, it was plain from the disappointed look on Mr. Blanker's face that no bird's-eye maples had been found. In his anger, Mr. Blanker even accused the Indians of switching trees! He looked greedily at the Indians' land, but we did not move. Finally the last tree was loaded onto the wagon and the team of horses pulled Mr. Blanker and the other men away.

I stood there looking at the stumps. The space in the air where the trees had once stretched would long be empty.

11

Spring arrived with the shrieks of returning seagulls. The hawks came back and then an eagle. One misty day there was a yellow rush of little warblers. I began to feel sorry for Icarus. He was shut up in the house away from all the other animals. For several days I put off what I had to do. Finally I took Icarus outside, kissed him, and let him go. He leaped up onto a nearby oak tree and clung to the trunk, looking down at me. I held my breath. Soon he was gliding from tree to tree. And then he was gone. I waited a long while, but he did not come back. I knew that I had been right to let him go, but that didn't make it any easier.

Early in May, Ke che gaw baw returned from the north. He had come to find a bride. Fawn said he was full of stories of the country around Kitchi-Gami. "He talks of the many animals in the woods where they live. He says they can walk for two days on land that no one owns."

The Indians of La Croix were busy cultivating the land they had bought. "They would rather be hunting in the woods like Ke che gaw baw than doing women's work in the field," Fawn told me.

"But they won't follow the others north, will they?" I asked. I was afraid that Fawn and her family would go away again.

"No. They would not leave their sacred burial ground. Besides, our chief says the white man follows the Indian like his shadow. Soon he will claim the land where Ke che gaw baw has made his new home."

One afternoon when I visited the camp

with Papa, I saw Ke che gaw baw. He was dragging a deer toward one of the wigwams. Papa said, "He is showing the family of the girl he courts that he is a good hunter and can provide for a wife."

All afternoon Fawn and I helped the women spread the nets for fishing. As we returned to the village, I heard what sounded like the sweetest of bird calls. It was unlike any birdsong I had heard before.

Fawn smiled. "It is Ke che gaw baw playing his courting flute. He has stood outside of White Deer's wigwam with his flute for many days."

"Doesn't White Deer's family want her to marry Ke che gaw baw?" I asked.

"Oh, yes, but it would not be proper for them to agree quickly."

Fawn took me along with her to gather mushrooms. The leaves on the trees were no larger than the ears of a mouse. The sun poured down onto a carpet of wildflowers. They were pushing up through drifts of last year's leaves. "We must look for mushrooms," Fawn said, "like this one and this." Fawn snatched at two mushrooms poking up from the ground. They were the exact color of the brown leaves.

I reached for some bright orange mushrooms, but Fawn stopped me. "You must be careful," she warned. "Those mushrooms will cause death." After a little while I became better at finding the good mushrooms. But I decided to leave the gathering to Fawn.

Tired from our searching, we sat down to rest in a patch of flattened grass. My friendship with Fawn was often a silent one. Fawn waits a long time between words. Only the songs of the returning birds made the woods noisy. Suddenly we saw a movement in the tall grass. We held our breaths, waiting to see what was hidden there.

What we saw were three puppies. Except for a patch of gray on their heads, the pups were all black. As we watched, they tussled with one another, touching noses, nipping at one another's ears, and tumbling over one another. A gray shadow moved through the grass. The shadow limped. It was our wolf! I jumped up and ran toward the pups, anxious to hold them. I was sure the wolf would welcome us. But as I came closer, its hackles stiffened. I heard a low, threatening growl and then the wolf lunged at me. It would surely have snapped its jaws around my wrist if Fawn had not pulled me away. We ran toward the Indian village as fast as we could, never looking behind us.

On the ride back home with Papa I told him what had happened. He gave me a stern look. "You must never get near wild animals, Libby, especially when they have young ones."

"But the wolf must have known us. She was *our* wolf."

"The wolf was doing just what animals are supposed to do," Papa said. "She was protecting her young." I thought of the picture in the Bible of the Garden of Eden. In the picture the wild animals all have smiles on their faces and follow Adam and Eve around like puppies. Now I understood that our woods was no Garden of Eden.

We did not see the wolf or her pups again. I thought of them often that summer. The pups would be learning to hunt. Little by little, their land would be taken from them. One day, like Ke che gaw baw, the wolves would seek wilder land and disappear from here forever.

Ke che gaw baw and White Deer were to be married. The tribe invited us to come to the marriage ceremony.

On the day of the wedding we traveled through sunlight. The small pale green leaves, budding on the trees, hardly made any shade at all. "Happy is the bride the sun shines on," said Mama. She had brought her paints. Our wedding gift to White Deer and Ke che gaw baw would be their portraits.

We arrived to find the whole village astir.

Earlier that morning White Deer and Ke che gaw baw had gone to the church in La Croix to be married. Now it was time for a large feast.

Papa talked with the chief and Sanatua while Mama got out her paints. Many of the Indians gathered around her to watch. I went to find Fawn. She was with the women who were preparing the feast. Sticks had been split at the top and fish tucked into the slots.

The sticks were stuck into the ground next to the fire to cook. Grouse and ducks also roasted on sticks. They gave off a funny smell, for they were cooked with their feathers on. Haunches of deer were roasting. Corn and squash were cooking in maple syrup. There was so much food that I did not see how even the whole village could eat it all. But they did and I helped.

Because everyone was so full, the dancing

began slowly. But soon the drums beat faster. There was much good-natured teasing of White Deer and Ke che gaw baw. Only White Deer's mother and father were quiet. They knew that in another day their daughter would leave the village to go to Ke che gaw baw's home. Most likely they would not see her again.

The chief raised his hands for silence. He looked like a king with his long silver earrings and beaded headdress. He spoke in the Ottawa language, so I could not understand him. Fawn said that he was giving a blessing to White Deer and Ke che gaw baw. "He is saying we have much to celebrate this year, for the tribe now owns the land we need." Fawn smiled at me. "He thanks your father."

After the talk there was more dancing, but Mama said it was time to take William home. I was sorry to leave and did not think it fair that I had to go just because William was sleepy. On the way back the moon lit the trail for us. We could hear an owl hooting.

Somewhere in the dark, Icarus was gliding among the trees.

That summer other settlers began to buy land around us. We heard the sound of axes chopping and trees falling. I was afraid Papa would think of leaving La Croix. When the land became too crowded, Papa had moved from Virginia to Saginaw, and then from Saginaw to the woods of northern Michigan. But Papa seemed content. I believe it was the lake.

We were often on the beach that summer. I walked along the shore looking for a special stone that had little eyes all over it. It reminded me of bird's-eye maple. Papa said such stones were very old. William sat at the edge of the water and let the little tongues of the waves lick his toes. Mama painted pictures of the lake. In her watercolors the sky and the lake melted into one blue puddle. Papa stood looking out across the water, happy that we could not see to the end of it.

About the Author

GLORIA WHELAN says, "Some years ago, like Libby and Fawn, my family moved to the woods of Northern Michigan. We canoe down the same streams the Indians canoed; the roads we travel each day were once Indian trails. It's not surprising, then, that the stories of the Indians should find their way into my imagination and my books."

Shadow of the Wolf is the third book in Gloria Whelan's critically acclaimed pioneer series. She has written many popular books for children, including *Next Spring an Oriole* and *Night of the Full Moon*. She lives with her husband in Northern Michigan.

About the Illustrator

TONY MEERS lives in Toronto, Canada with his wife and four children. He loves illustrating children's books because he remembers how much he enjoyed the pictures in his favorite childhood books. "I always looked for books with exciting illustrations that carried me away to other places and times. The pictures made the story more magical, and made me think of the world as a place with endless possibilities."